My Favorite Red Sneakers

EARLENE CONNER

My Favorite Red Sneakers

iUniverse books may be ordered through booksellers or by contacting:

iUniverse
1663 Liberty Drive
Bloomington, IN 47403
www.iuniverse.com
1-800-Authors (1-800-288-4677)

Because of the dynamic nature of the Internet, any web addresses or links contained in this book may have changed since publication and may no longer be valid. The views expressed in this work are solely those of the author and do not necessarily reflect the views of the publisher, and the publisher hereby disclaims any responsibility for them.

Any people depicted in stock imagery provided by Getty Images are models, and such images are being used for illustrative purposes only.
Certain stock imagery © Getty Images.

ISBN: 978-1-5320-5068-8 (sc)
ISBN: 978-1-5320-5065-7 (e)

Library of Congress Control Number: 2018906722

Print information available on the last page.

iUniverse rev. date: 08/03/2018

My Favorite Red Sneakers

One morning before school Timmy over heard his mommy talking on the phone; as he was getting ready for school.

When Timmy got done he ran into his mom room and asked, Mommy who where you talking too? She replied back; your favorite Aunt Helen.

Timmy got very excited! He asked; is she coming for a visit? She said yes. Timmy had a big smile on his face and hugged his mommy. Timmy Said she always brings me presents. I wonder what she is going to bring me this time mommy. His mother said well I don't know Timmy we will just have to wait and see.

Aunt Helen arrived after Timmy went to school.

When Timmy got home he seen his Aunt Helen and his eyes lit up and he smiled and said Aunt Helen" you are here. She said yes Timmy and gave Timmy a big hug. She Said Timmy look what I have for you. Aunt Helen said I brought you a special gift". Timmy seen A nice size shoe box wrapped package, and he said is this for me........ Aunt Helen said yes for my Special nephew.

Aunt Helen said here Timmy open it. So Timmy opened his present and inside were red sneakers. Timmy said oh boy; Thanks Aunt Helen. Aunt Helen said now lets' try them on Timmy to see if the sneakers fit. So Timmy put them on and they were a perfect fit.

Timmy jumped up and down with joy and hugged and kissed his Aunt Helen and said thank you for my sneakers Aunt Helen;. I love them. Timmy mom Sarah said thank you also to Helen and told Timmy the sneakers looked good on his feet. Well it was dinner time for everyone.

Daddy just got home for work and immediately Timmy ran to his dad and said look daddy notice anything different about me? His dad picked little Timmy up in his arms and said; no Timmy. What is different? Timmy said look at my feet Aunt Helen bought me new sneakers! He said excitedly. Dad said wonderful Timmy they look awesome on your feet. Dad asked Timmy how do they feel. Timmy said great dad. I think that I can run fast now and jump really high. Dad said; Hold on now Timmy, these sneakers are not magic.

So they went into the kitchen and daddy greeted his sister Helen and thanked her for the sneakers and making Timmy's day. They all sat down at the table and begin to eat dinner, and Timmy was so happy he couldn't stop talking about the sneakers that his Aunt Helen had given him and they were his favorite color.

Well 2 days had went by and it was time for Aunt Helen to leave and she was packing to leave in the spare room. Timmy knocks on the door. Aunt Helen says come in. Timmy opened the door and stood in front of Aunt Helen and told her how much he loved her and was going to miss her after she leaves to go back home. Aunt Helen told Timmy how much she loved him and how much she was going to miss him, but she told Timmy that she will be back for Christmas. After all Aunt Helen never had any kids so it pleased her to do a lot for Timmy; it also brightened up her world.

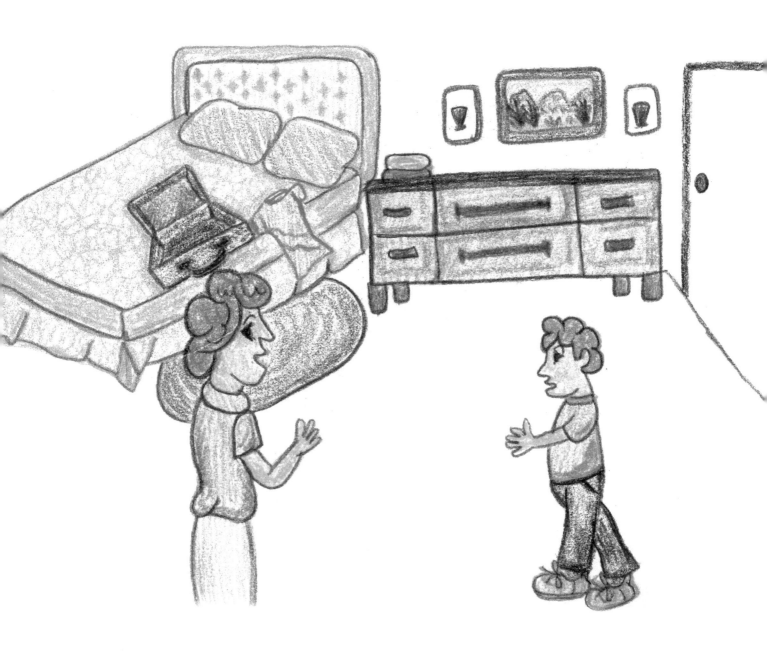

So Timmy said; come on Aunt Helen I will walk you down the stairs and see you to your cab. Helen sad thank you Timmy you are much the gentleman. My brother and your mother has taught you well. So down the stairs they went. Helen said her good byes' to everyone and got into the cab and left.

So now hours had went by and it was time for Timmy to say goodnight to his parents. He had to go to school in the morning. Time went by pretty fast it was time for Timmy to get ready for school.

Timmy got on the bus and went to school wearing his new red sneakers his Aunt Helen had given him. He couldn't wait to tell the teacher about his new sneakers.

The Teacher told Timmy she think they looked great and that red was her favorite color.

Well when it was time for recess Timmy felt that the sneakers made him run faster and jump higher. He felt like a Super Hero.

Timmy ran a relay race against Jack and he never beat Jack before until now.

Timmy looked down at his sneakers and said to himself WOW! I can run fast. Then it was time to play kickball and it was Timmy's' turn to kick.

Johnny rolled the ball to Timmy and Timmy kicked that ball past Johnny clear out in the center of the playground and then Timmy ran as fast as he could. He got on every base and then to home plate without anyone getting that ball to get him out. Timmy was safe and scored a home run in kickball. Timmy was so excited and all the kids on his team was excited for him as well. At this moment Timmy was convinced that the shoes had to be magic.

Well it got later in the day around 3:00pm time to get on the bus and go home. Timmy couldn't wait to tell his parents how special his sneakers were. When Timmy got off the bus and ran into the house his mommy greeted Timmy and said hello Timmy how was school? Timmy went on to say how his recess went today at school, about how he ran and won the relay race between him and Jack, and how he never beat Jack before. Then he told his mom about the kickball game how he kicked a homerun and everyone was happy and excited about him playing. Timmy said; mommy I think my sneakers is magic. Timmy mom said well I don't know about magic but I think maybe you feel that way because your favorite Aunt Helen gave them to you and it was a special gift from her to you. Timmy said; but mommy my sneakers made me feel like a Super Hero or something, they just got to be magic. Timmy mom replied back and said maybe there just special sneakers.

Later on Timmy went outside to play with his dog Spot and two of his friends Jack and Johnny. Well time has passed, dinner was over and bedtime had come.

Timmy got ready for bed and took of his clothes and sneakers. Timmy put the sneakers at the end of his bed on the floor.

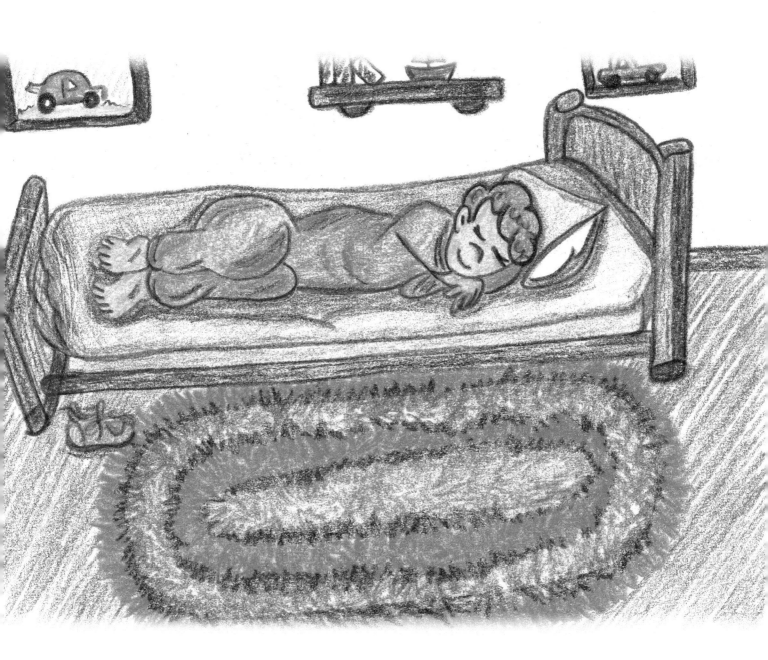

Morning had come time for school, so Timmy get out of bed put on his clothes his mother had laid out for him and when he looked for his sneakers one was missing.

Timmy yelled and asked his mommy where his other sneakers was. Timmy mom said' I don't know. Where did you put them? Timmy said at the foot of his bed on the floor. His mom said okay Timmy we don't have much time before you catch the bus. Lets' look for it.

She told Timmy to check the closet, and under the bed. Timmy did, no sneakers.

Timmy mother looked in the toy box and in the hamper. No sneakers. Timmy mom said well Timmy you just going to have to wear your old shoes. Timmy said but mom I can't go to school without my sneakers. They make me run fast and jump high. I won't be any good at recess without my favorite sneakers. Sarah said Timmy you got to do the best you can for today.

So Timmy went to school sad and depressed. Timmy walked into his classroom with his head held down and a frown on his face. His teacher Miss Bee said Timmy what is the matter? Come over here and tell Miss Bee why you look so sad. Did anyone bother you before you came into our classroom? He said no mam. She said then what in the world is wrong? This isn't like you. Timmy said one of my favorite red sneakers is gone that my Aunt Helen gave me and I don't know where it is. Miss Bee said' did you look everywhere you think it might be? Like under your bed, or in your closet, the toy box? Timmy said yes and it isn't there. Miss Bee said well you go home later look again. So later in school it was time for recess. Timmy didn't want to play any games because he wasn't wearing his favorite red sneakers that made him run fast and jump high.

The kids tried their best to get him to play with them but Timmy wouldn't he was convinced that the sneakers made him better at everything that he wasn't good at before. Well Wendy seen Timmy sitting on the bench with his head down, she said come on Timmy I'm no good either. Come play with us. Timmy got up off the bench and tried having fun it was no use.

Well it was 3pm now school is out and Timmy on the bus going home. The bus pull up at the house, and Timmy got off the bus and his mother standing at the door waiting for him. Timmy looked up at her and said mommy did you find my shoe? No Timmy I didn't I'm sorry. Timmy's mom asked if he had homework to do. He said no he didn't. Timmy told his mother that he was going outside to play with spot, she said okay. So Timmy went outside and yelled at Spot. Spot come running and he jumped up on Timmy and they played and played. Then Spot went into his dog house and came back out with the red sneakers in his mouth.

Timmy was too excited to be mad at Spot, he got the sneakers and ran into the house and said mommy, mommy, look what I got! Timmy's' mom turned around and asked where did you find it? Timmy said I didn't Spot had it in his dog house.

Timmy's' mom remembered that Spot had come inside the house that night Timmy had to go to bed early, the night his Aunt Helen had left, so that had to be when Spot took his sneakers at the foot of his bed. So Timmy hurried up and put his sneakers on. He went outside and he ran and jumped and played like no other. Timmy was so happy that he got his sneakers back he felt like a Super Hero again.

So as time went by he wore those sneakers every day until one Friday came and Timmy was late and in a hurry to catch the bus and put the wrong shoes on. Timmy had a good day at school winning relay races, playing kickball and had so much fun. Even when he got home he played and still had fun. Running and jumping and everything. Timmy's mother noticed how he was having fun and playing well. Then came the time for Timmy to go to bed for the night. Well Timmy's mother tucked him in, and she said Timmy did you notice today what shoes you had on today" all day. Timmy said my sneakers. Timmy's mom said no Timmy she reached down beside her and picked up the shoes that Timmy was wearing and Timmy's eyes got big and he said" I couldn't have because I was running fast and jumping high and even won a relay race today at school.

Timmy's mom said" Timmy I think you wanted to believe in your heart and mind that the red sneakers that your Aunt Helen given you where magic because she is your favorite Aunt and she loves you as if you where her own son. Not only that you are small for your age and those sneakers in your mind made you feel special that you could do anything. At least that is what you told yourself and that's fine but the truth is you had it in you all the time to run fast, jump high and be good at sports and everything you want to do. The key was confidence. The sneakers' your Aunt Helen gave you was out of love, and when you put them on that's what gave you a boost. Timmy's mom said do you understand Timmy. Timmy looked up at his mom and said" I think so mom and thank you for explaining this to me, then Timmy said goodnight mommy I love you. So from then on as Timmy grew up, from that conversation his mom and him had when she tucked him in bed that night he knew that it wasn't the shoes or sneakers or the clothes you wear that makes you have special abilities because we all have special abilities it's up to us to bring them out in us.